Jessica Souhami studied at the Central School of Art and Design, and went on to set up a touring shadow puppet company, featuring music and a storyteller. She is internationally acclaimed for her folk-tale retellings, bringing some of the world's greatest stories to a young audience. Her many books for Frances Lincoln include *The Strongest Boy in the World*, *Foxy!*, *Sausages*, *King Pom and the Fox*, *The Sticky Doll Trap*, *The Little Little House*, *Old MacDonald*, *No Dinner!*, *The Leopard's Drum*, the classic West-African tale which has just celebrated its twentieth anniversary, and *Rama and the Demon King*. Jessica lives in north London.

HONK, HONK!
Hold Tight!

Jessica Souhami

Frances Lincoln
Children's Books

For Robert, with thanks for all the laughs.

About the Story

Stories about a princess who never laughs are widespread and have been told for centuries. They are particularly well known all over Europe, and an important early version is in Basile's Neopolitan *Il Pentamerone* of the seventeenth century. The hero who makes the princess laugh is always a poor, good-hearted young man who is then offered a great prize by the king – often the princess herself as a bride. I couldn't have that! It seems more likely to me that the princess would realise how great it would be to have a funny husband and that she would propose to him! A golden goose is the magical element of the story, and magical golden birds are found in stories as far back as the fourth century BC in the *Jataka Tales* of the birth stories of Buddha.

JANETTA OTTER-BARRY BOOKS

First published in Great Britain and in the USA in 2015 by Frances Lincoln Children's Books
This first paperback edition published in Great Britain and in the USA in 2016 by Frances Lincoln Children's Books
74-77 White Lion Street, London N1 9PF
QuartoKnows.com
Visit our blogs at QuartoKnows.com

Text and illustrations copyright © Jessica Souhami 2015

A CIP catalogue record for this book is available from the British Library.

ISBN 978-1-84780-541-6

Illustrated with collage of Ingres papers hand-painted with watercolour inks and graphite pencil

Printed in China

1 3 5 7 9 8 6 4 2

There was once a princess called Alice, who never laughed.

She never smiled the tiniest bit.

This made her father, the King, very sad.

"My poor Alice," he sighed. "How awful to live without laughter."

The King tried everything he could
think of to make her laugh…

But Alice remained glum.

The King thought for a very long time
and then he announced,

"I will share my kingdom with anyone
who can make Princess Alice laugh."

Many people tried — but they all failed.

Princess Alice was still gloomy.

The news reached a poor young man called Peter,
who decided to see this glum princess for himself.

He packed a loaf of bread and a bottle of wine
and set out for the palace.

After a while he saw an old woman wrapped in a huge black cloak, sitting by the roadside. She looked tired and hungry.

"Please, sir," she asked, "can you spare a crust and a drop to drink?"

"Of course," said Peter. "Take my loaf and wine. I'm young and strong and can do without."

As soon as these words were spoken,
the old woman swept aside her cloak…

AND REVEALED…

a beautiful goose with feathers of pure **GOLD**.

"You're a kind-hearted lad, Peter," said the old woman, smiling.
"Tuck this magic goose under your arm and carry it to the
palace, where you will be rewarded.

"BUT," she warned, "if anyone stretches out a
hand towards the goose, it will cry,

'**HONK,**

HONK!'

and you must call,

'Hold tight!'

See what happens then!"

The old woman chuckled and disappeared!

Peter was astonished.

But he picked up the goose and went on his way.

A young woman passing by looked at the magnificent goose.

"Mmm," she said to herself. "A gold feather would look wonderful
in my hat. No one would miss just one little gold feather."

She stretched out her hand to the goose's tail **AND...**

the goose cried,

"HONK, HONK!"

Peter called,

"Hold tight!"

And the young woman could not pull her hand free!

She was stuck fast to the goose and had to follow on behind Peter.

A man stretched out his hand
to help the young woman,
and guess what?

YES!

The goose cried,

"HONK, HONK!"

Peter called,

"Hold tight!"

And the man could
not pull free. He had
to follow too!

In the same way, Peter collected a baker delivering buns.

She laughed and pointed to the man and…

"HONK, HONK!"

"Hold tight!"

She was stuck.

Then a clown who reached for a bun…

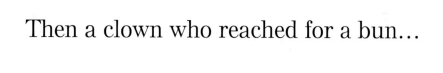

"HONK, HONK!"

"Hold tight!"

A butcher's boy who
wanted a balloon…

"HONK, HONK!"

"Hold tight!"

And a small dog who smelled sausages…

This odd chain of people and dog **scrambled and shambled** behind Peter, higgledy-piggledy all the way to the palace.

Princess Alice just happened to look out of her window as they passed.
And when she saw this comical bunch…

she smiled,

she chuckled,

she laughed

until her sides ached.

And suddenly…

...the spell was broken!

The magnificent magical goose disappeared,
and the people came unstuck and scurried home.

The King was delighted.

He hugged Peter and thanked him again and again.

And so, as promised, the King shared the kingdom with Peter.

After some time, Princess Alice thought how good it would be to have a husband who made her laugh.

"Will you marry me, Peter?" she asked.
And Peter said,

"Yes!"

And they lived merrily ever after.

OTHER TITLES BY JESSICA SOUHAMI FROM
FRANCES LINCOLN CHILDREN'S BOOKS

The Strongest Boy in the World

Kaito is stronger than all the other boys in his village. Because no one can beat him at wrestling, he sets off to the city to compete in the world-famous Sumo wrestling tournament. But on the way he meets a most extraordinary girl… Can Hana help puny little Kaito become the strongest boy in the world?

'This is a beautiful retelling of an old tale, enriched by action-packed illustrations that capture the humour and bring the story and characters to life.'
– *English Association*

ISBN 978-1-84780-603-1

Foxy!

"Don't look in the sack!" says Foxy. But everyone just has to have a little peep. Crafty Foxy tricks them all – and into his sack go a fine rooster, a fat pig, and even a little boy! Can anyone put a stop to Foxy's wicked plan? Luckily the last woman Foxy meets is as clever as he is…

'An excellent spin on a familiar trickster story' – *Kirkus Starred Review*

ISBN 978-1-84780-498-3

Rama and the Demon King

Banished by his jealous stepmother, the good and brave Prince Rama has lived in the forest for 14 years, along with his beautiful wife Sita and his loyal brother Lakshaman. Rama has triumphed over the demons that dwell there and the three live a simple, peaceful life among the forest animals. But it is not to last, for the ten-headed King of the Demons vows to take revenge…

'This 3000-year-old story is still appealing today, especially when, as here, it is retold in such exuberant style' – *Parents In Touch*

ISBN 978-1-84780-660-4

Frances Lincoln titles are available from all good bookshops.
You can also buy books and find out more about your favourite titles,
authors and illustrators on our website: www.franceslincoln.com